RAINBOW magic™

Olympia the Games Fairy was originally published
as a Rainbow Magic special. This version has
been specially adapted for developing readers
in conjunction with a Reading Consultant.

Special thanks to
Narinder Dhami
and Sarah Levison

Reading Consultant: Prue Goodwin, lecturer in literacy and children's books.

ORCHARD BOOKS
Carmelite House, 50 Victoria Embankment, London EC4Y 0DZ
Orchard Books Australia
Level 17/207 Kent Street, Sydney, NSW 2000

This text first published in 2012 by Orchard Books
This Early Reader edition published in 2016
© 2016 Rainbow Magic Limited.
© 2016 HIT Entertainment Limited

HiT entertainment

Illustrations © Orchard Books 2016

A CIP catalogue record for this book is available from the British Library.

ISBN 978 1 40834 199 5
1 3 5 7 9 10 8 6 4 2

Printed in China

MIX
Paper from
responsible sources
FSC
www.fsc.org
FSC® C104740

The paper and board used in this book are made from wood from responsible sources

Orchard Books is an imprint of Hachette Children's Group and published by
the Watts Publishing Group Limited, an Hachette UK company.

www.hachette.co.uk

Olympia
the Games Fairy

by Daisy Meadows

ORCHARD

www.rainbowmagic.co.uk

Fairy Stadium

Melford

The river

Otter
holt →

Jack Frost's
Ice Castle

Cycle route

Running route

Winners' podium

Contents

Story One

The Sparkling Swimming Cap

Chapter One

Swimming Surprise

"This is going to be really exciting!" Kirsty Tate said, smiling at her best friend, Rachel Walker.

Kirsty was staying with Rachel for the summer holidays. Today they were

going with Rachel's parents to
a special sports event called
a triathlon!

"It's going to be great,"
smiled Rachel. "The
competitors take part in
swimming, cycling and running
races, one after the other!"

Mr Walker parked the car
and they all followed the
crowds to a wide river.

"Ladies and gentlemen,"
boomed a voice from a
loudspeaker. "The triathlon
will begin in five minutes!"

"Mum, could Kirsty and I watch the race from the riverside?" Rachel asked.

Mrs Walker nodded. "We'll see you back here later," she told them.

Kirsty and Rachel found a quiet spot near a clump of reeds.

"I wonder if we'll see our fairy friends this summer?" Rachel said hopefully.

"Oh, I hope so!" Kirsty exclaimed. She and Rachel were friends with the fairies,

and together they'd had some
amazing adventures!

At that moment there was the
sound of a whistle.

All the swimmers jumped into the river to start the race. But, right away, something very strange started to happen. The athletes all suddenly spun around in the water and began heading the wrong way!

A sparkle in the river caught Rachel's eye, and she nudged Kirsty.

"One swimmer seems to be OK," Rachel said. She pointed at a boy in a dazzling silver swimming cap.

At that moment there was another announcement over the loudspeaker.

"Attention, everyone!" it boomed. "The race will be postponed while we carry out some checks."

Just then, Kirsty gasped. The reeds next to them were glowing! A moment later, a tiny fairy appeared.

"Hello, girls," she called as Rachel and Kirsty smiled. "I'm Olympia the Games Fairy!"

Chapter Two

A New
Fairy Friend!

Olympia fluttered up in the air,
her golden hair sparkling in the
sunlight.

"I'm so glad to see you, girls!"
Olympia exclaimed. "I've just
come from the Fairyland Games,
and everything's in a mess."

"The Fairyland Games?"

Kirsty asked. "What are those?"

"We have swimming, cycling and running competitions," explained Olympia. "I have three magical objects to help me look after these events, and the same sporting events in the human world.

The sparkling swimming cap looks after all swimming events. My musical bicycle bell ensures cycling races run smoothly. Finally, the tireless trainers make sure that all running events are enjoyable!"

"So what happened?" Kirsty asked.

Olympia sighed. "In the swimming event, all the competitors began swimming around in circles! And that's when I discovered my sparkling swimming cap was missing."

"The swimming event has gone wrong here too, Olympia!" Rachel cried.

Olympia frowned. "I must find the sparkling swimming cap," she said. "I can feel it's nearby!"

"We'll help you look for it," Rachel said.

As Kirsty looked at the river, she spotted the boy in the shiny swimming cap. Then she saw he had a long green nose!

"Olympia!" Kirsty cried, "that's a goblin, and he's wearing your sparkling cap!"

Olympia peered at the river. "You're right!" she declared. "I'll turn you into fairies, and then we'll fly out and grab the cap."

Olympia pointed her wand at the girls. They felt themselves shrinking to fairy size with gauzy wings!

The three friends zoomed off. But a boat reached the goblin swimmer before them!

"Oh, no!" Rachel exclaimed. "There are three more goblins on the boat!"

"It's my turn to wear the sparkling swimming cap now," one of the goblins yelled.

"No, it's not!" cried the goblin swimmer.

The goblin on the boat leaned
over and grabbed the sparkling
swimming cap from the goblin's
head.

The other two goblins on
the boat rushed over. They all
wanted to wear the cap!

As they squabbled, the cap fell into the river.

"Now's our chance!" Olympia cried.

But as the fairies swooped down, Kirsty spotted an otter heading straight for the sparkling swimming cap. The otter grabbed the cap in her teeth and swam off with it!

Chapter Three

Inside the
Otter's Den

"Girls, follow that otter!"
Olympia cried.

The three friends whizzed
after the otter. She soon
scrambled out of the water and
slipped into a hole.

"She's gone into her holt,"

said Olympia. "That's what an otter's home is called. Let's follow her."

The three friends flew down the tunnel after the otter. They soon reached the heart of the otter's den.

The creature had placed the swimming cap on the ground, in front of five adorable baby otters!

Rachel fluttered forwards. "Excuse me, but that swimming cap belongs to our friend. And she would really like it back. It's very important, you see!"

"I'm sorry," the otter replied, "but I'm going to use it as a comfy bed for my babies!" Olympia, Kirsty and Rachel came up with a plan.

Olympia fluttered forwards.

"If you give us the cap back," she said softly, "I'll magic up the most comfortable bed for you all!"

The otter thought hard.

"That's very kind of you," she said. "You can have your swimming cap back."

Olympia tapped the sparkling swimming cap with her wand

and it shrank down to its
Fairyland size. Next she waved
her wand and a cosy nest of
moss and grass appeared!

The little otters gave squeaks
of delight.

"Thank you!" the mother
otter said gratefully.

Waving goodbye, Olympia
and the girls flew out of
the holt and into the bright
sunshine.

"Girls, thank you so much for
your help," Olympia said with
a huge smile.

"I must return the cap to Fairyland so that the swimming event can start."

"Can Kirsty and I stay as fairies for a little while?" Rachel asked.

"Of course," Olympia agreed. "I'll come back soon and change you back to your human size!"

As Olympia disappeared, another announcement boomed from the loudspeaker.

"Attention, everyone! The race will restart in five minutes."

"Great!" Rachel said happily. "We've saved the first event of the day!"

Kirsty smiled. "You're right, but I'm sure we haven't seen the last of those naughty goblins!"

Story Two

The Musical
Bicycle Bell

Chapter One

Bicycle Breakdown!

"Wasn't that amazing?" Rachel said with a grin.

The swimming race had just finished. The first few swimmers were out of the water and were getting ready for the bicycle race.

Kirsty and Rachel were still fairy-sized and they were perched on a house near the start of the cyclists' route.

The girls watched as the first athlete climbed onto his bike. He pedalled off quickly. But he'd only gone a little way when his bike began to wobble from side to side. Then his handlebars fell off his bicycle!

"Oh, no!" cried Kirsty and Rachel.

Most of the swimmers were now on their bicycles.

But as they pedalled off, everything was going wrong. Seats fell off the bikes and crashed to the ground. Wheels and handlebars came loose and some of the bicycles even started to go backwards!

"Attention, everyone!" The announcer's voice boomed from the loudspeaker. "The race has been stopped. We hope to restart in ten minutes."

"This must be to do with those naughty goblins," Rachel sighed.

"I think you're right, Rachel!" Kirsty replied. "And look, there's Olympia!"

Their fairy friend came flying out of a loudspeaker in a haze of sparkles.

She zoomed towards the friends, looking very worried.

"Hello, girls!" she cried. "The goblins have stolen my musical bicycle bell! That's why all cycling events have been disrupted. Will you help me find it?"

"Of course we will!" Kirsty and Rachel said excitedly.

The three fairies flew away from the crowds and into a quiet lane.

"The goblins will be super cyclists now that they've got the musical bicycle bell," Olympia sighed.

Suddenly, five cyclists
whizzed down the lane where
Rachel, Kirsty and Olympia
were hiding. As they passed by
the fairies, the friends saw that
the cyclists had green faces!

"Goblins!" Kirsty breathed.
The goblin in the lead rang
the silver bell on the front of
his bicycle. The sound of a
beautiful melody filled the air.

Grab That Bell!

"That goblin has my musical bicycle bell!" Olympia cried. "After him, girls!"

Olympia, Rachel and Kirsty set off after the goblins. But the green racers were travelling very quickly!

The
goblin with
Olympia's
bell rang it
again as he
flew around
the next
corner.

"You've
had the bell for ages,"
one of the other goblins
complained. "It's my turn!"

"Come and get it then!" the
first goblin jeered. He cycled off
as fast as he could.

"You know Jack Frost wants the silly bell so that he can win the cycle race," shouted one of the goblins. "Don't lose it!"

"So Jack Frost told his goblins to steal my bell so that one of them can cheat and win the race!" Olympia cried. "Girls, we have to stop them!"

They followed the goblins into the busy streets. The goblin at the back of the pack picked up a stick and poked it through the leading goblin's front wheel.

The bicycle came to a sudden halt, and the goblin went flying over the handlebars and landed in the road!

A race official, who'd been standing on the corner of the lane, rushed towards the goblins.

"What are you doing?" he demanded. "The race hasn't restarted yet!" He glared down at the goblin on the ground. "And it's against the rules to ring your bell so loudly! I'm going to confiscate it."

The official removed the musical bicycle bell and slipped it into his pocket.

"Oh, no!" Olympia gasped, horrified. "What shall we do now, girls?"

Chapter Three

Ring a Ling Ding!

"I have an idea!" Kirsty exclaimed suddenly. "Maybe we can make the official throw the bell away…and then we can take it back!"

"How?" asked Rachel.

"By making the bell ring and ring without stopping!"

Kirsty turned to Olympia. "Could you do that with your magic?"

Olympia nodded. She pointed her wand at the race official. A stream of sparkles danced through the air towards his pocket.

Immediately the air was filled with the sound of the musical bicycle bell. The official pulled the bell out of his pocket in surprise. He tried everything he could think of to turn it off, but it wouldn't stop!

The official quickly hurried over to a nearby litterbin and threw in the bicycle bell.

The fairies zoomed down towards the litterbin.

"Look out!" Kirsty gasped  as she saw the goblins also rushing over to the bin. As they reached it, the goblins banged their heads together!

Olympia swooped down and grabbed the musical bicycle bell. The moment she touched the bell it stopped ringing and shrank down to its original Fairyland size.

Olympia fluttered upwards with a smile, clutching the bell. One goblin tried to catch her, but he missed and knocked the bin over. The rubbish flew out and covered the goblins!

"Give us back the bell!" one goblin roared.

Olympia shook her head.

"Go home and tell Jack Frost that he shouldn't try to win races by cheating!" she told them.

The goblins all slouched away grumpily, leaving their bicycles behind.

"I can't thank you enough for all your help," Olympia smiled. "Now the cycling races here and in Fairyland will be able to go ahead!"

"Ladies and gentlemen," the announcer said in a happy voice over the loudspeaker,

"the bikes have been fixed and we can now restart the race!"

"Oh, great!" Rachel smiled. "Everything is back to normal."

"Would you like to come to Fairyland with me to return the bell?" asked Olympia.

"We'd love to!" they beamed, and Olympia waved her wand.

Story Three
The Tireless Trainers

Chapter One

Ready, Steady but NOT go!

Moments later, Olympia, Rachel and Kirsty were in the Fairyland sports stadium!

"Rachel and Kirsty have helped me find the musical bicycle bell!" Olympia announced. The fairies all cheered loudly.

There were three plinths
in front of the royal box. The
sparkling swimming cap sat
on one stand, and the dazzling
tireless trainers were on the other.
Olympia carefully placed the
musical bicycle bell on the empty
plinth.

"Hello, girls,
and hello,
Olympia,"
King Oberon
called. "Please
join us for the
running race!"

Olympia, Rachel and Kirsty sat down in the front row. Bertram the frog footman stepped onto the running track and smiled.

"Our contestants today are the Rainbow Fairies!" Bertram announced.

The seven Rainbow Fairies went over to the starting line.

Bertram cleared his throat. "Ready! Steady!" He paused. "GO!"

The Rainbow Fairies set off and the crowd cheered.

But suddenly Ruby and
Amber both fell over.

"Our laces have been tied
together!" Amber yelled.
Meanwhile, Fern and Sky were
trying to pull their trainers off.

"They're too small!" Sky said.
The other three fairies stopped
running too as strange things
happened to their trainers!

Samantha the Swimming Fairy ran over to Rachel and Kirsty. "Jack Frost has stolen the tireless trainers!" she cried.

"Oh, no!" Olympia said. "What shall we do now?"

"Don't worry, Olympia," Kirsty said. "Rachel and I will help you to get them back."

Rachel nodded. "I'm sure Jack Frost has taken them to his Ice Castle!"

Olympia and the girls flew together out of the stadium and over the lush meadows and sparkling rivers of Fairyland.

Soon they saw Jack Frost's castle looming ahead of them. The doors began to open.

The three friends hid behind one of the icy turrets. Peering out, they saw Jack Frost come running out of the castle. On his feet were the tireless trainers!

Jack Frost's goblins looked very worried.

"Do something!" Jack Frost roared furiously as he ran around in circles.

"What's happening?" Rachel whispered, puzzled.

"It's the powerful magic of the tireless trainers," Olympia explained. "Jack Frost can't stop running!"

Terrible
Trainers!

"Get these terrible trainers off
my feet!" Jack Frost bellowed at
the goblins.

"We're going to catch you
with a net!" one of the goblins
explained.

They tried to hurl a net over
him. But at the last moment,

the tireless trainers sent him scooting away in the opposite direction. The net fell over two nearby goblins!

Two other goblins tried to rugby tackle Jack Frost but they just ran into each other.

"How are we going to get the trainers back?" Rachel asked with a frown. "Jack Frost isn't going to slow down!"

Jack Frost looked up and spotted the three fairies hovering above him.

"Come down and help me!" Jack Frost panted furiously.

"Only if you return the tireless trainers," Olympia replied.

Jack Frost scowled. "NO!" he yelled. Then he pointed his ice wand at the trainers, zapping them with his magic.

"Don't!" Olympia called. "Your magic won't stop them!" But Jack Frost took no notice. Suddenly, an ice bolt whisked him out of sight. "Jack Frost's magic has taken him to the human world!" Olympia cried. "Let's follow him!"

With one wave of her wand,

a burst of fairy magic carried the three friends back to where the triathlon was being held.

"Look, the running race has almost finished," Rachel said. There was a crowd of runners heading towards the finish line.

"And there's Jack Frost!" Olympia exclaimed.

Rachel and Kirsty could see Jack Frost running along with the other athletes. To their dismay, they saw all the other runners stumbling and having problems with their trainers!

Jack Frost shot out in front.

"Jack Frost is going to win!" Kirsty cried.

Sure enough, Jack Frost crossed the finish line first.

"I won!" he boasted. "Clever old me!"

"You there!" One of the race organisers strode over to Jack Frost. He looked very cross. "You appeared in the middle of all the other runners right at the end. You're disqualified!"

A Very Special Medal!

Jack Frost looked very sulky indeed. The tireless trainers meant he couldn't stop moving and so he ran furiously up and down on the spot.

"Well, what a very eventful triathlon this has been!" the judge said with a smile.

"We're going to present our winners with their medals now, but first we have a special prize to present. This prize is for

'Bad Sport of the Day'!"

The judge pointed at Jack Frost, who was still bouncing in his trainers. "Would you come and collect your prize, please?"

Jack Frost's face lit up. "I am a winner!" he yelled happily. He dashed forwards and the judge handed Jack Frost a large cabbage!

Jack Frost was delighted. Clutching his cabbage, he ran off down the street.

Olympia and the girls flew to catch up with him.

When they did, Rachel could see that he was very tired.

"Please help me!" Jack Frost gasped. "I'll give you these terrible trainers if only you can get them off my feet!"

"Very well," Olympia agreed. "The only thing is, I don't know how to take the trainers off." She turned to Rachel and Kirsty. "Any ideas, girls?" she asked hopefully.

Kirsty stared down at the tireless trainers. Suddenly, she had an idea!

"Can you do a handstand up against that wall?" she asked the Ice Lord. "Then we should be able to untie the trainers and take them off your feet."

Jack Frost ran over to the wall and then flipped himself up into a handstand. Now he was still running, but in midair!

The three fairies dodged around Jack Frost's waving feet. Working together, they managed to pull off both of the trainers. They immediately shrank down to their Fairyland size.

Jack Frost gasped with relief
as he flipped himself upright
again. "Phew!" he groaned.
"I'm going home for a nap!"
Then he waved his wand and
an ice bolt carried him away.

"Girls, you were amazing!"
Olympia smiled. She gave
Rachel and Kirsty a huge hug
and turned them back into
humans again.

Then, holding the tireless trainers, Olympia disappeared in a sparkling mist of fairy dust.

"Wasn't that the most exciting competition ever?" Rachel said, as she and Kirsty ran to watch the medals ceremony.

"It was," Kirsty replied with a smile. "Thanks to Olympia and our fairy friends!"

The End

**If you enjoyed this story,
you may want to read**

Alexandra the Royal
Baby Fairy
Early Reader

Here's how the story begins…

"Are we nearly there, Mum?"
asked Kirsty, leaning as far
forwards in the car as her
seatbelt would let her.
"We can't wait to get to the
palace!"

Mrs Tate turned her head
a little to smile at Kirsty and
her best friend, Rachel Walker.

They were sitting side by side in the back of the car.

"Not long now, girls. When we reach the top of this hill you'll be able to see Norwood Palace straight ahead. Look, there it is!"

The girls gasped as they saw a beautiful building ahead of them. It was made from golden stone and surrounded by smart gardens.

"Wow!" cried Rachel as the car pulled into the drive.

Rachel was staying with her

best friend Kirsty for the spring half-term holidays. Mrs Tate was a volunteer at Norwood Palace and today the girls were going to help with a children's open day.

Read
Alexandra the Royal Baby Fairy
Early Reader
to find out what happens next!